FUNNYMAN MEETS THE
MONSTER FROM OUTER SPACE

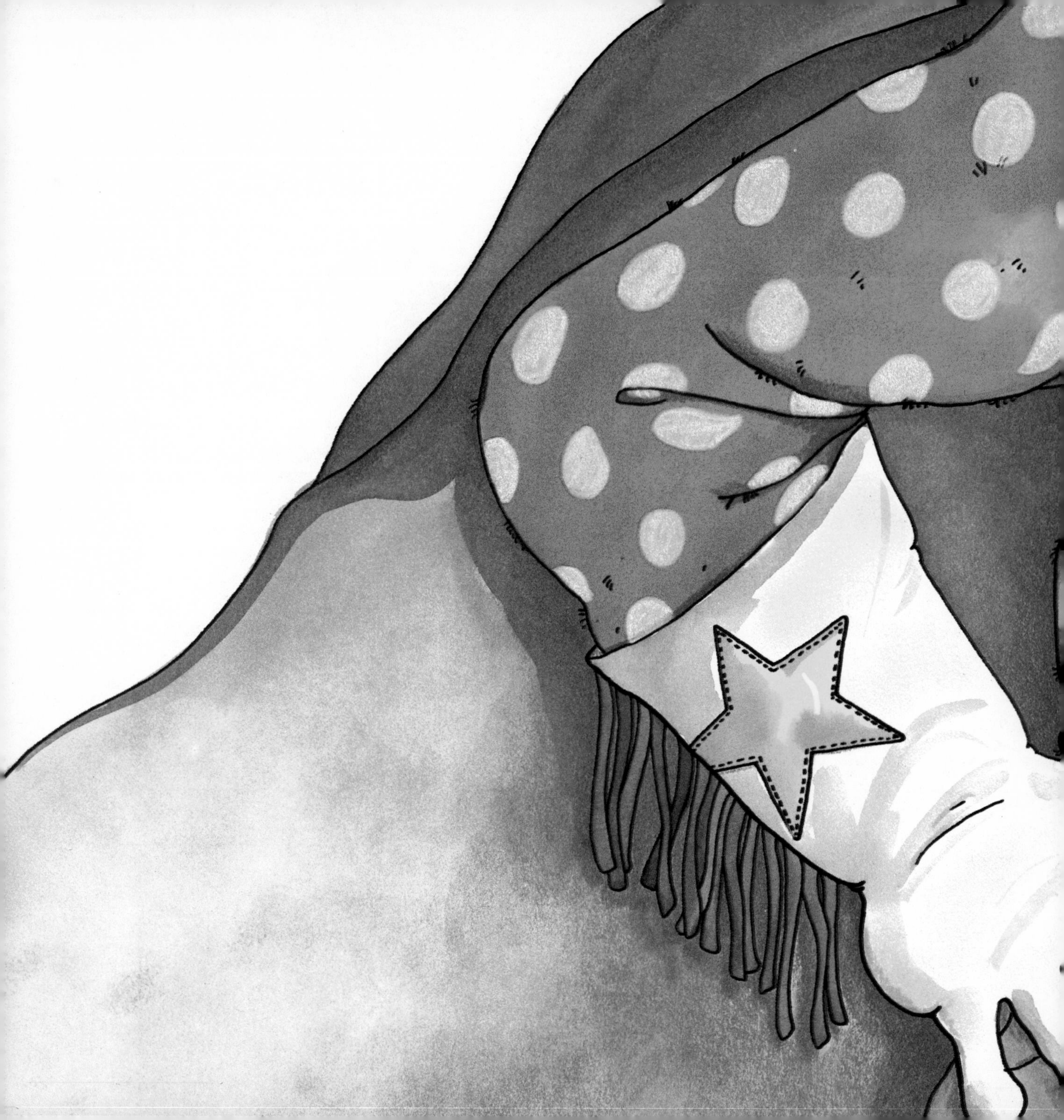

FUNNYMAN
MEETS THE
MONSTER FROM OUTER SPACE

by Stephen Mooser
pictures by Maxie Chambliss

SCHOLASTIC INC.
New York Toronto London Auckland Sydney

For Pat Mercier Mooser
—S.M.

For Sahara, Mugsey,
and Sam
—M.C.

ISBN 0-590-33959-1

Art direction by Diana Hrisinko. Text design by Sarah McElwain

12 11 10 9 8 7 6 5 4 3 2 1 7 8 9/8 0 1 2/9

Printed in the U.S.A. 24
First Scholastic printing, April 1987

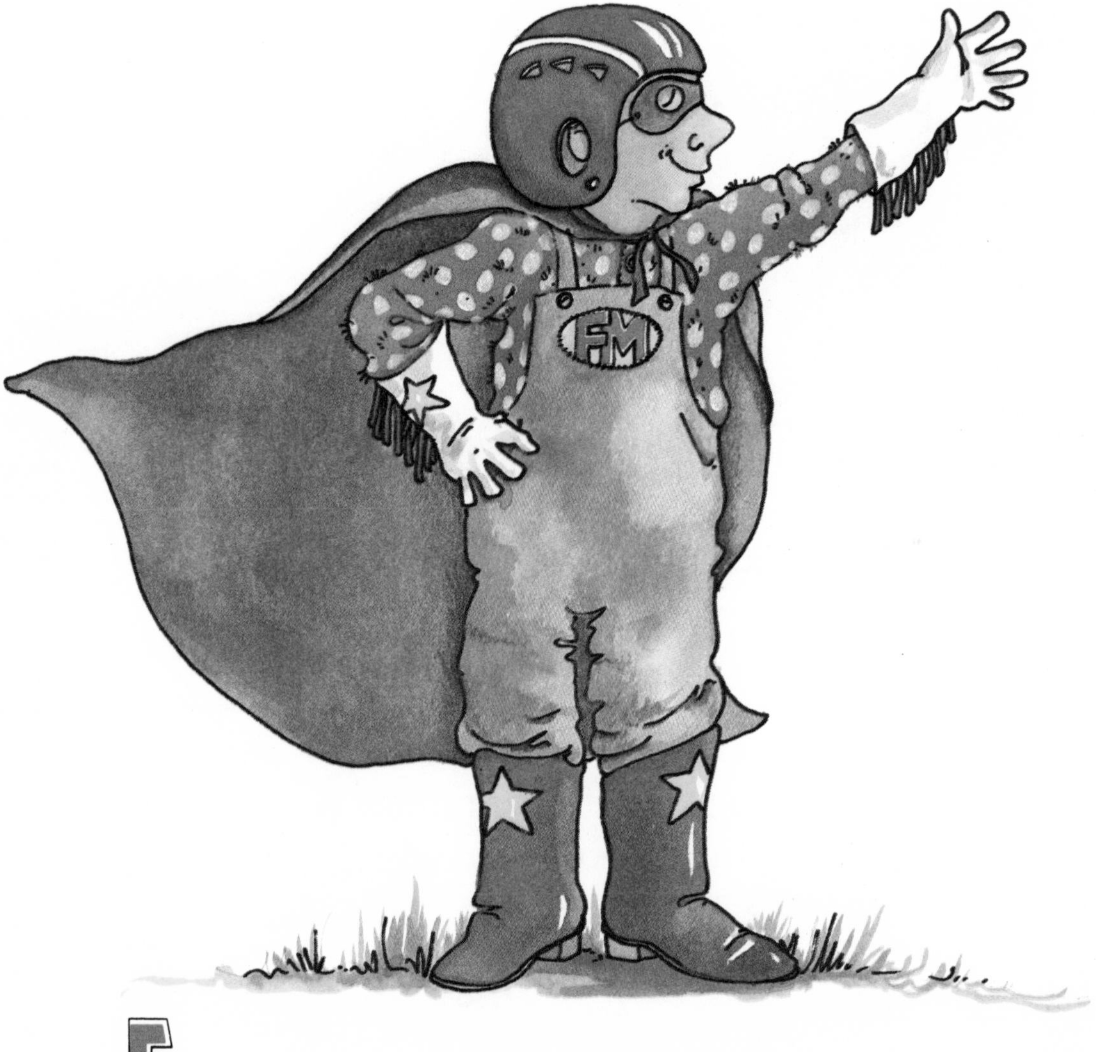
FM

Funnyman was a very famous detective. He was the only man in the world who stopped crime with jokes.

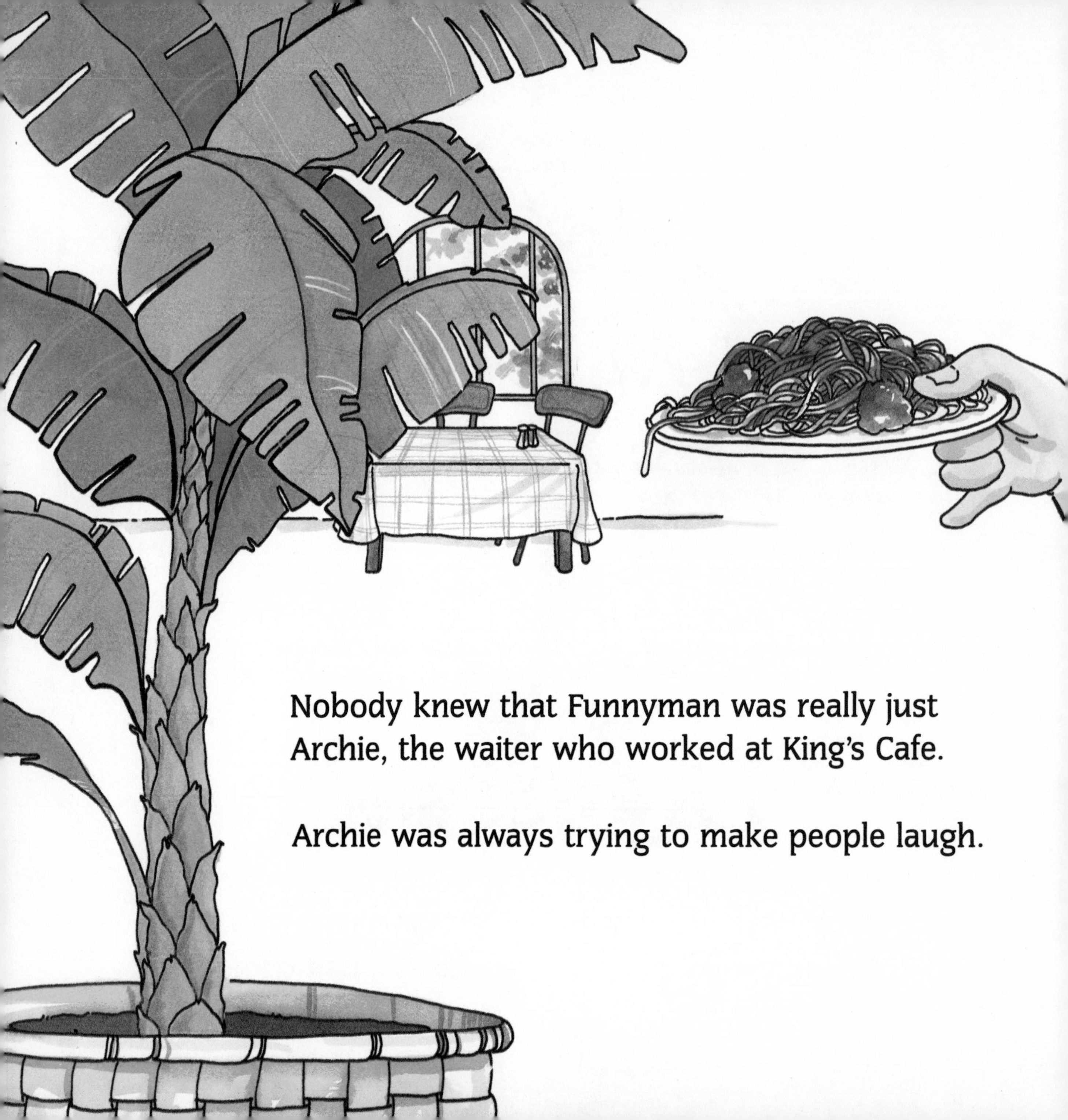

Nobody knew that Funnyman was really just Archie, the waiter who worked at King's Cafe.

Archie was always trying to make people laugh.

One day, he heard a woman say to a girl,
"If you'll be good, I'll give you a quarter."

"A quarter!" said Archie. "Why, when I was a little boy, I was good for nothing!"

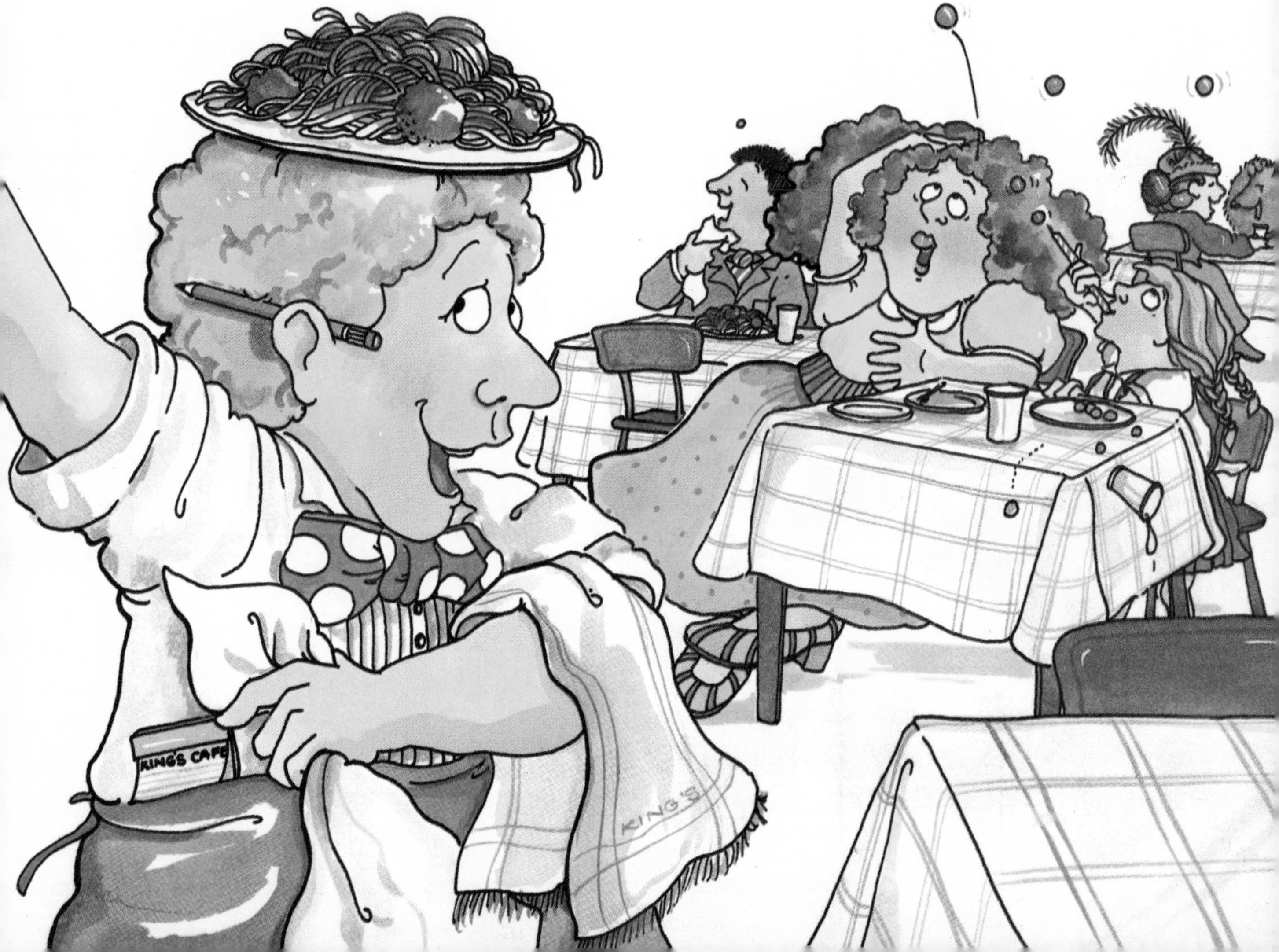
KING'S
KING'S

While everyone was laughing, Archie saw something that wasn't very funny. It was Mr. Crown, who owned the bank across the street. He was standing in front of the bank. And he was crying.

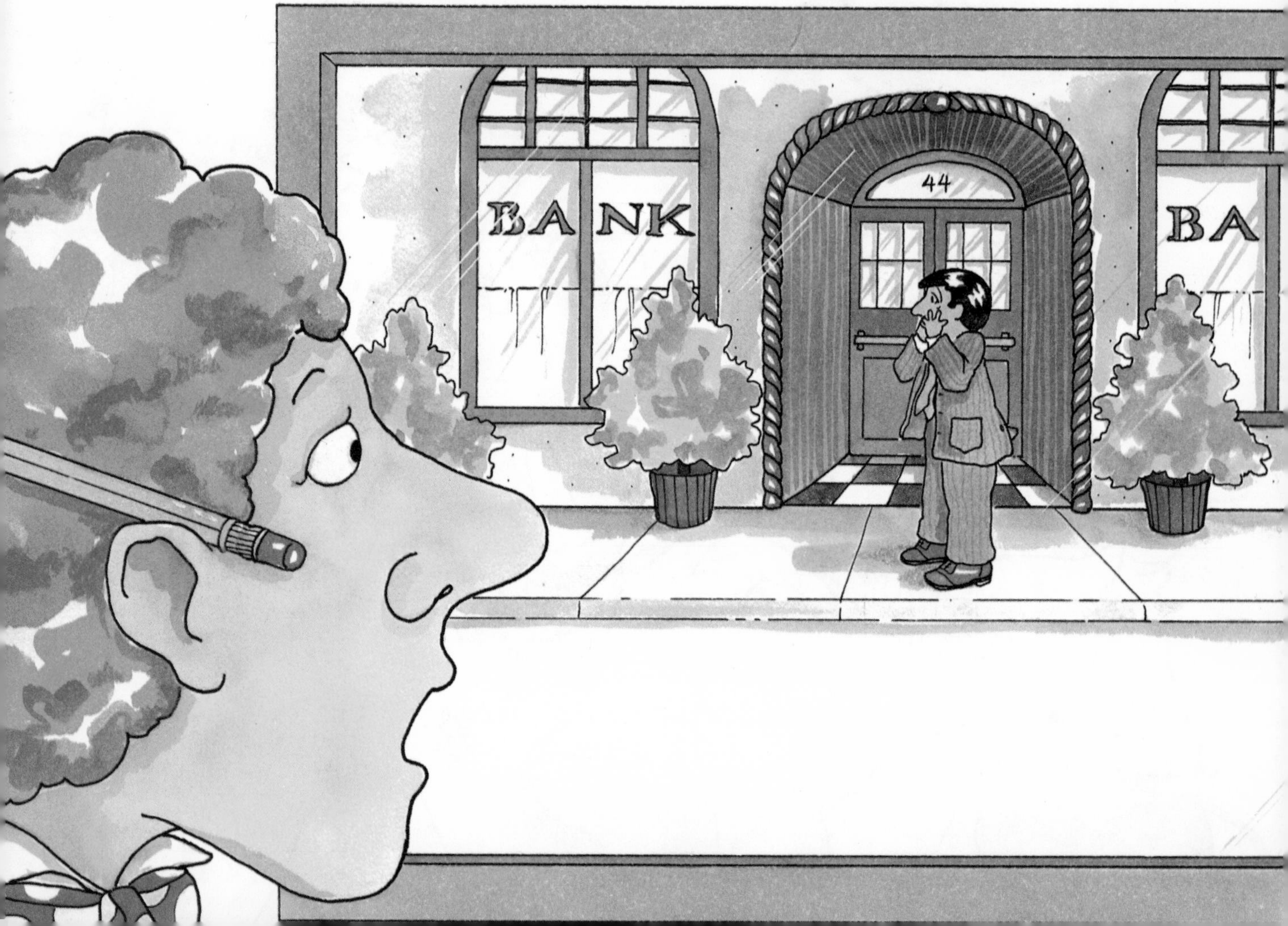
BANK
44
BA

"This looks like trouble," said Archie. "I think it's a job for Funnyman."

In a wink, he went into a back room and changed into his Funnyman disguise. Then he ran across the street.

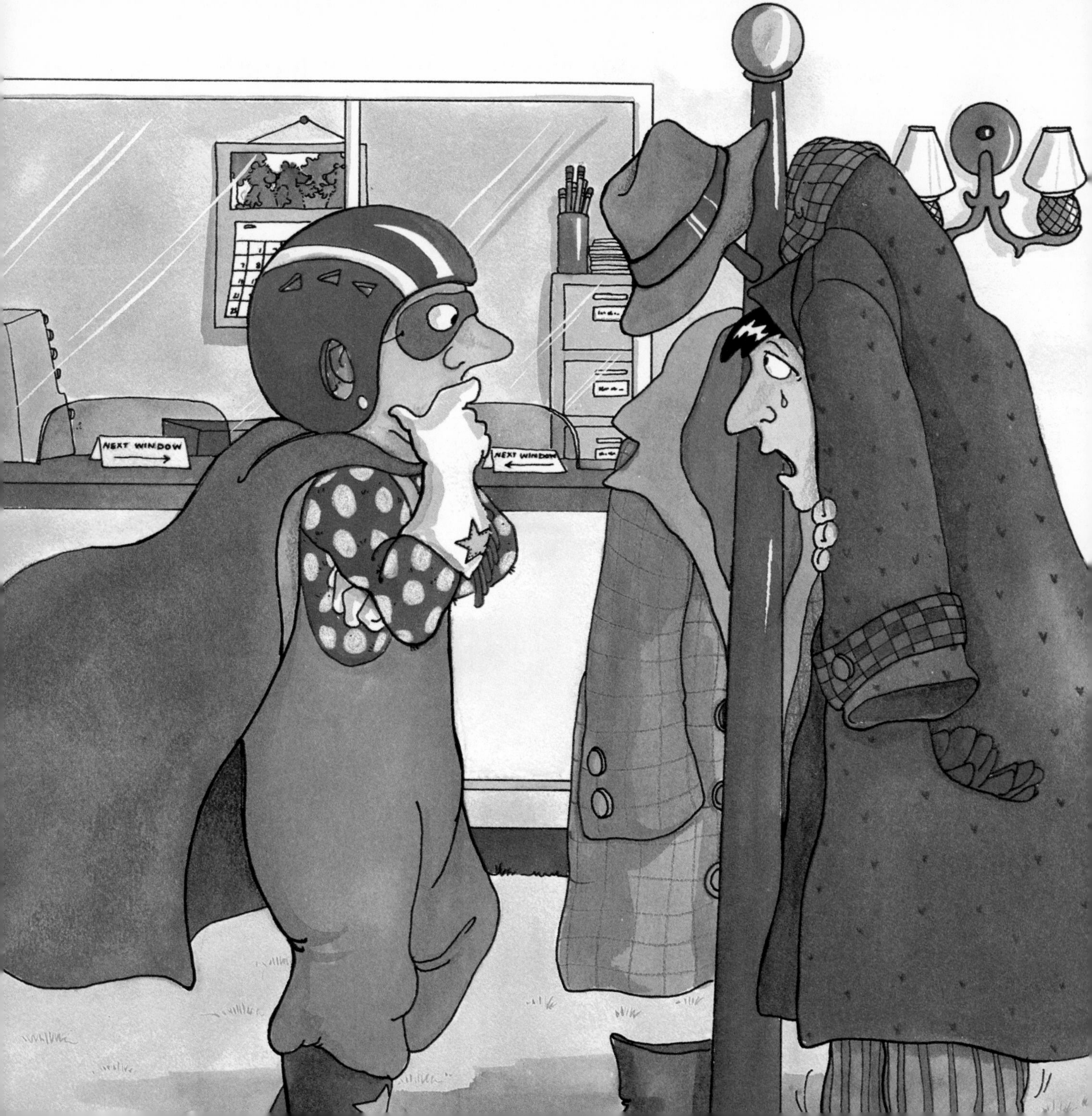
NEXT WINDOW
NEXT WINDOW

"Funnyman!" said Mr. Crown. "Am I glad to see you! Did you have the TV on this morning?"

"No," said Funnyman. "This morning, all I had on were my pajamas."

"No, no. I mean, did you see the news about Baldy McLain?" said Mr. Crown.

"What happened?" asked Funnyman.

"Baldy has been robbing banks all over the state. I'm afraid he's going to rob me next," said Mr. Crown.

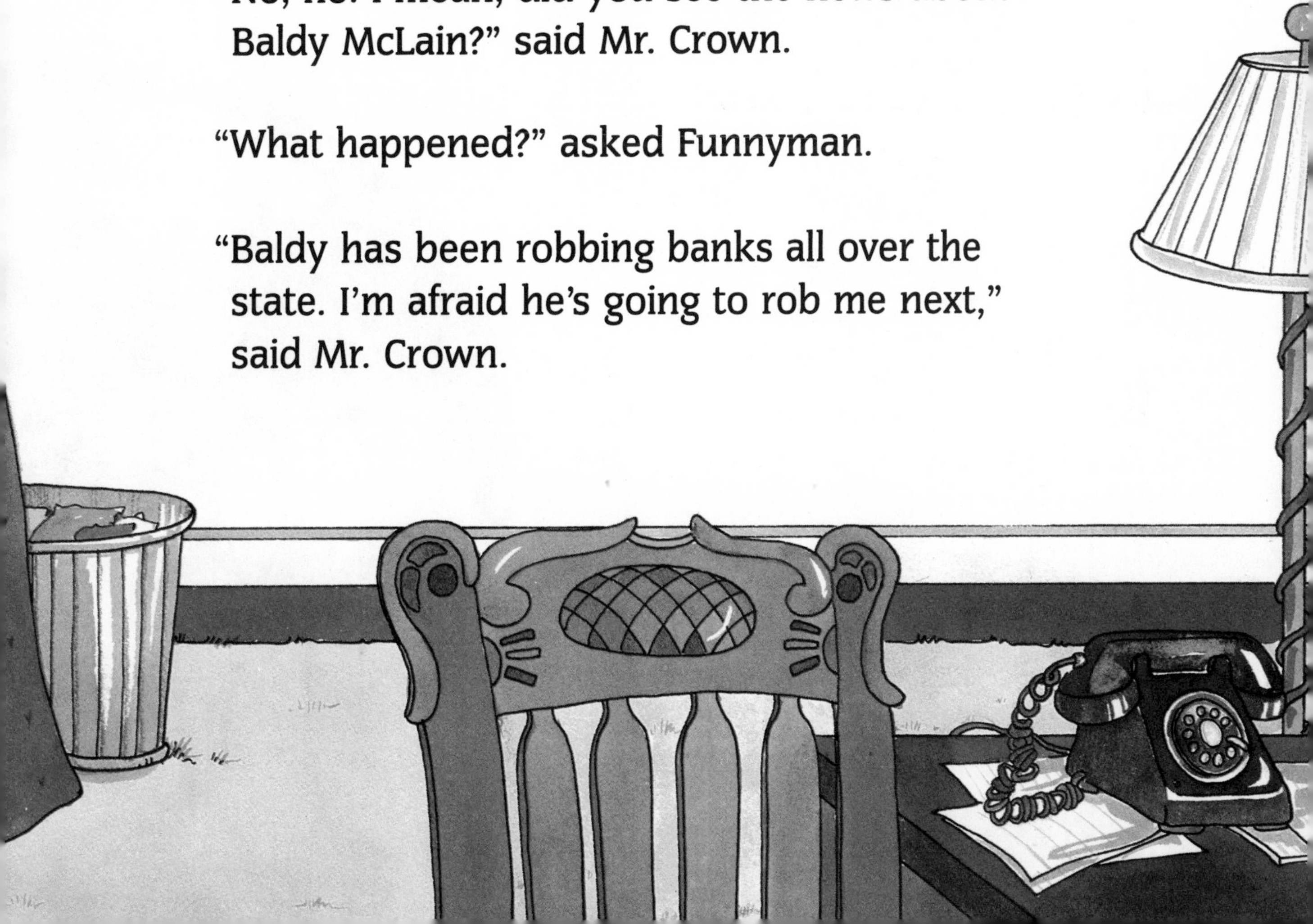

"That's terrible," said Funnyman.

"I need your help," said Mr. Crown. "Are you busy today?"

"No, today I'm Funnyman," said the famous detective.

"Must you always tell jokes?" said Mr. Crown.

"That's my job," said Funnyman. "Remember, I'm the guy who stops crime with jokes."

"Then, please, help me stop Baldy," said Mr. Crown.

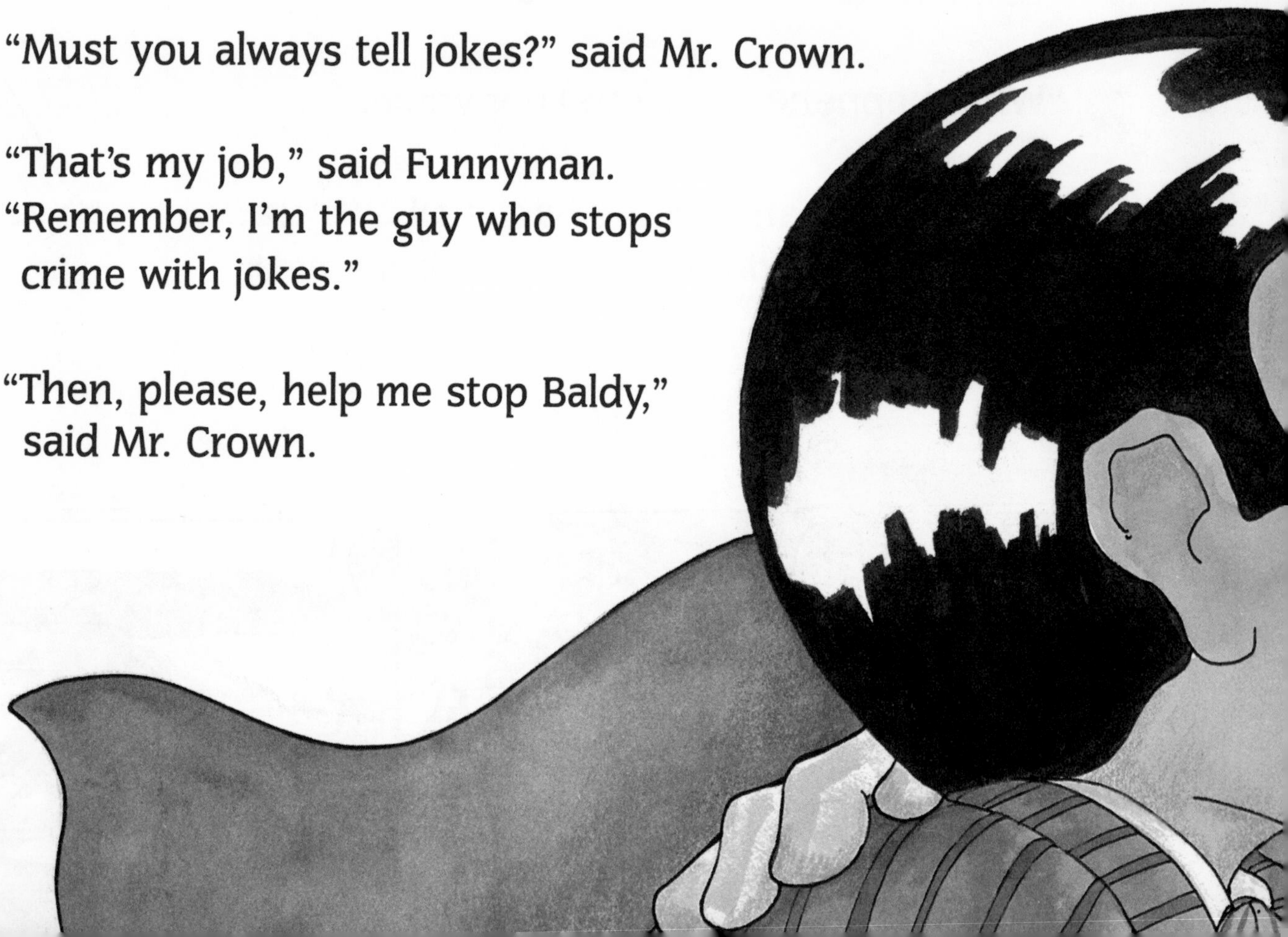

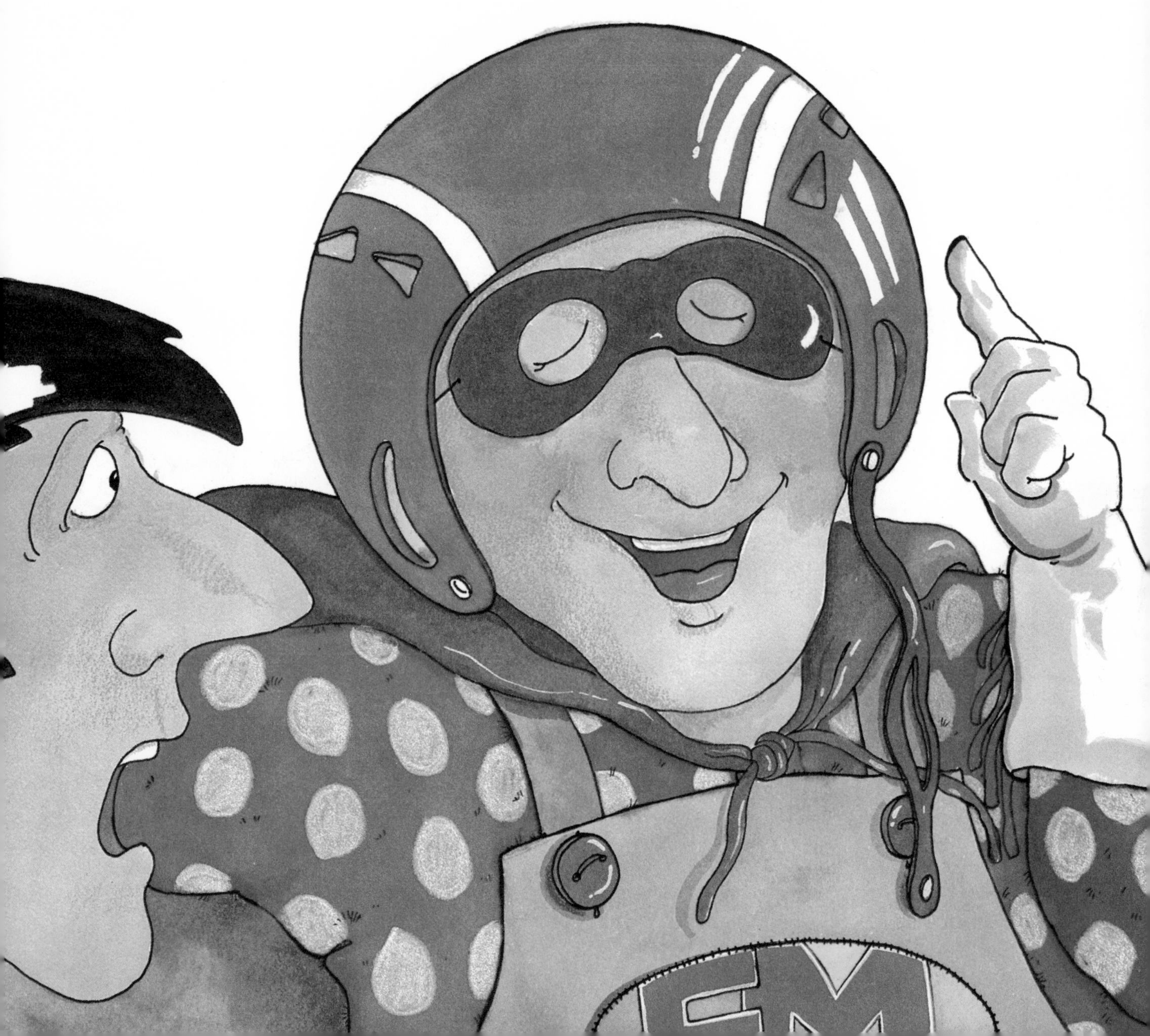

Before Funnyman could answer, a frightened boy came running into the bank.

"An invader from space!" he yelled. "A monster is coming down the street. Run! Run for your lives!"

Funnyman and Mr. Crown went outside. The whole town was running away. "What's going on?" asked Funnyman.

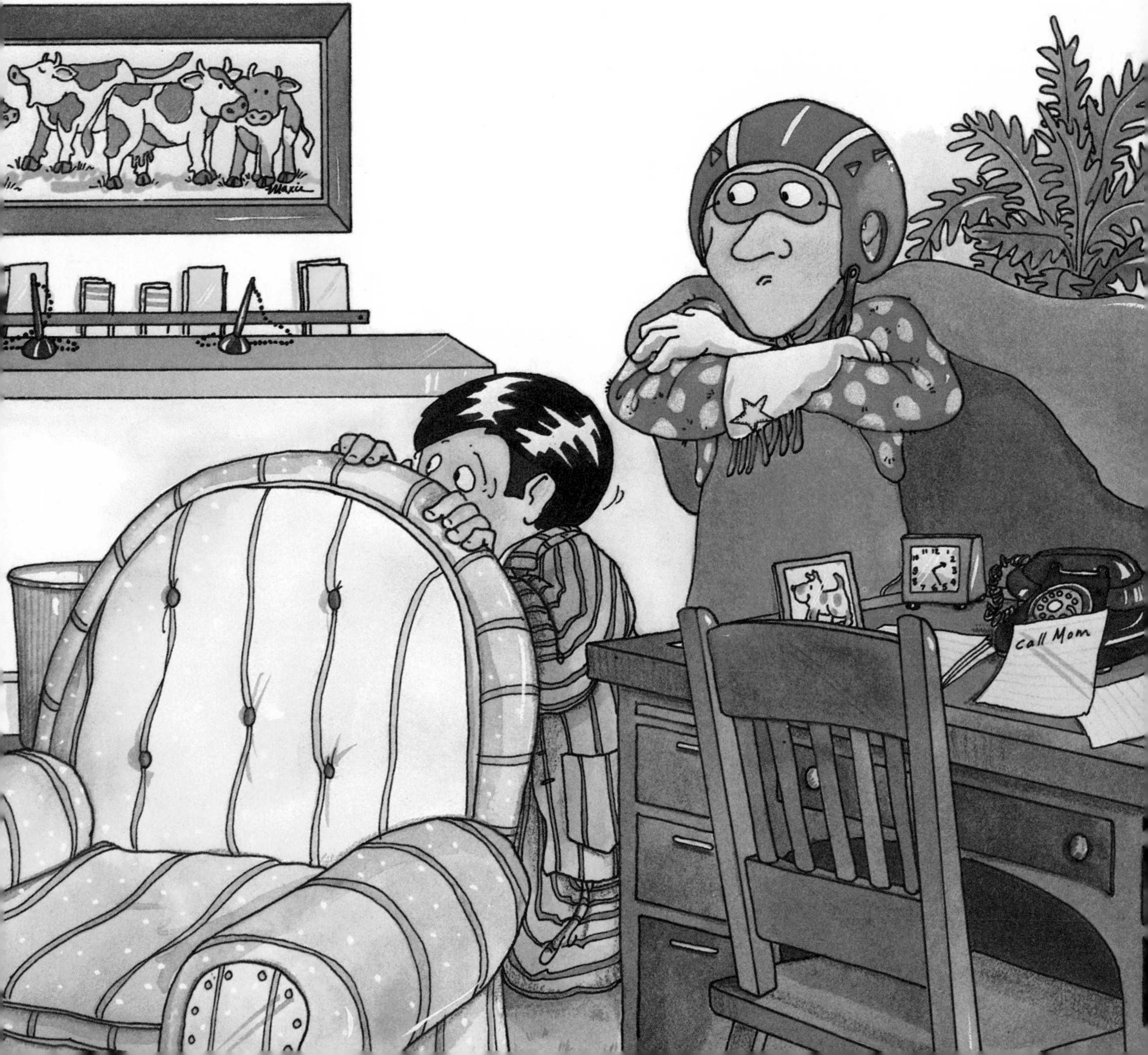
Call Mom

"A creature from Saturn has landed," said a woman. "He told us to get out of town."

"And he told us, if we didn't get out he would turn us into frogs," said a man.

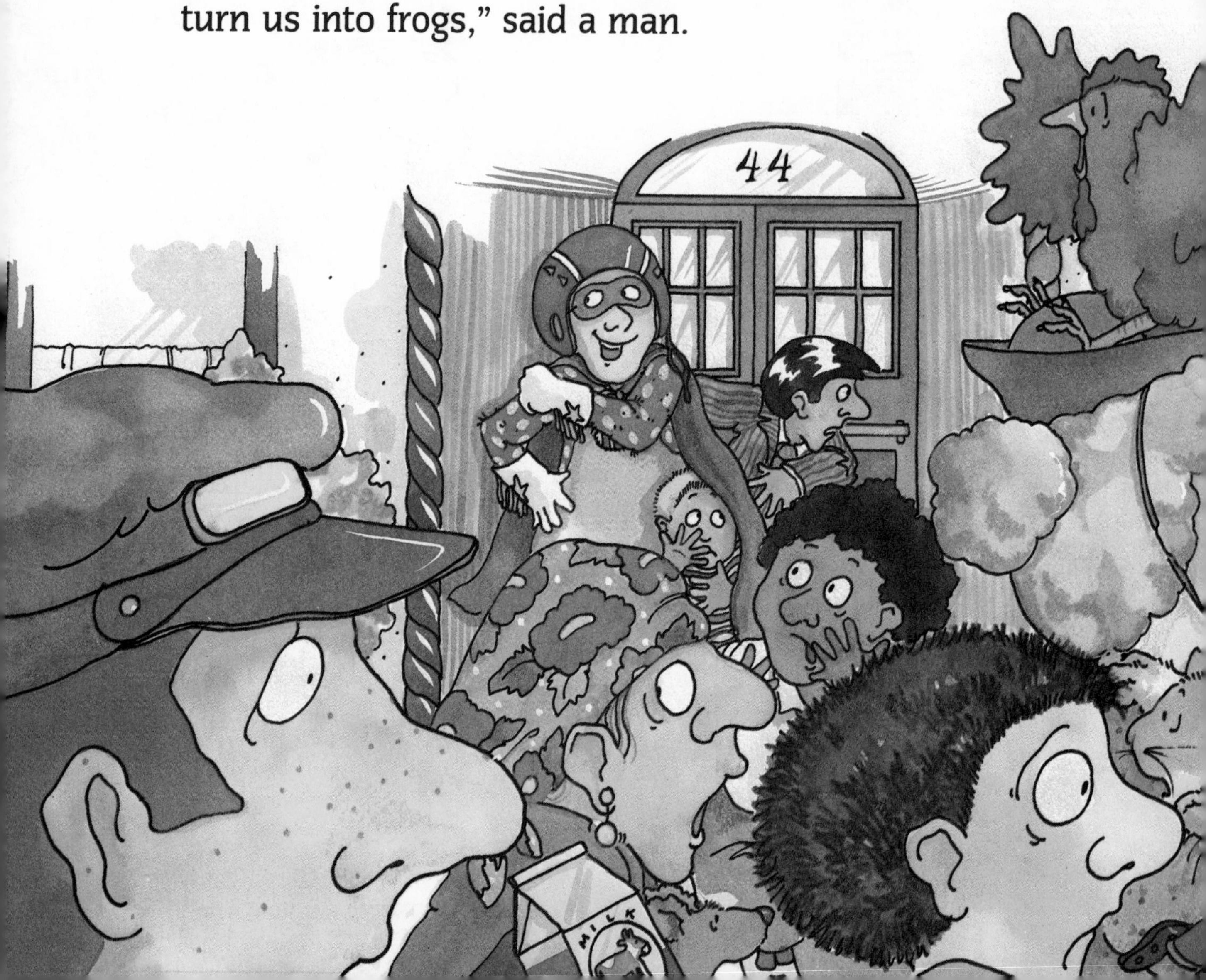
44
MILK

“If he did that to me, I’d be hopping mad,”
Funnyman smiled.

“This is no time for jokes,” said Mr. Crown.
“We’d better get out of here.”

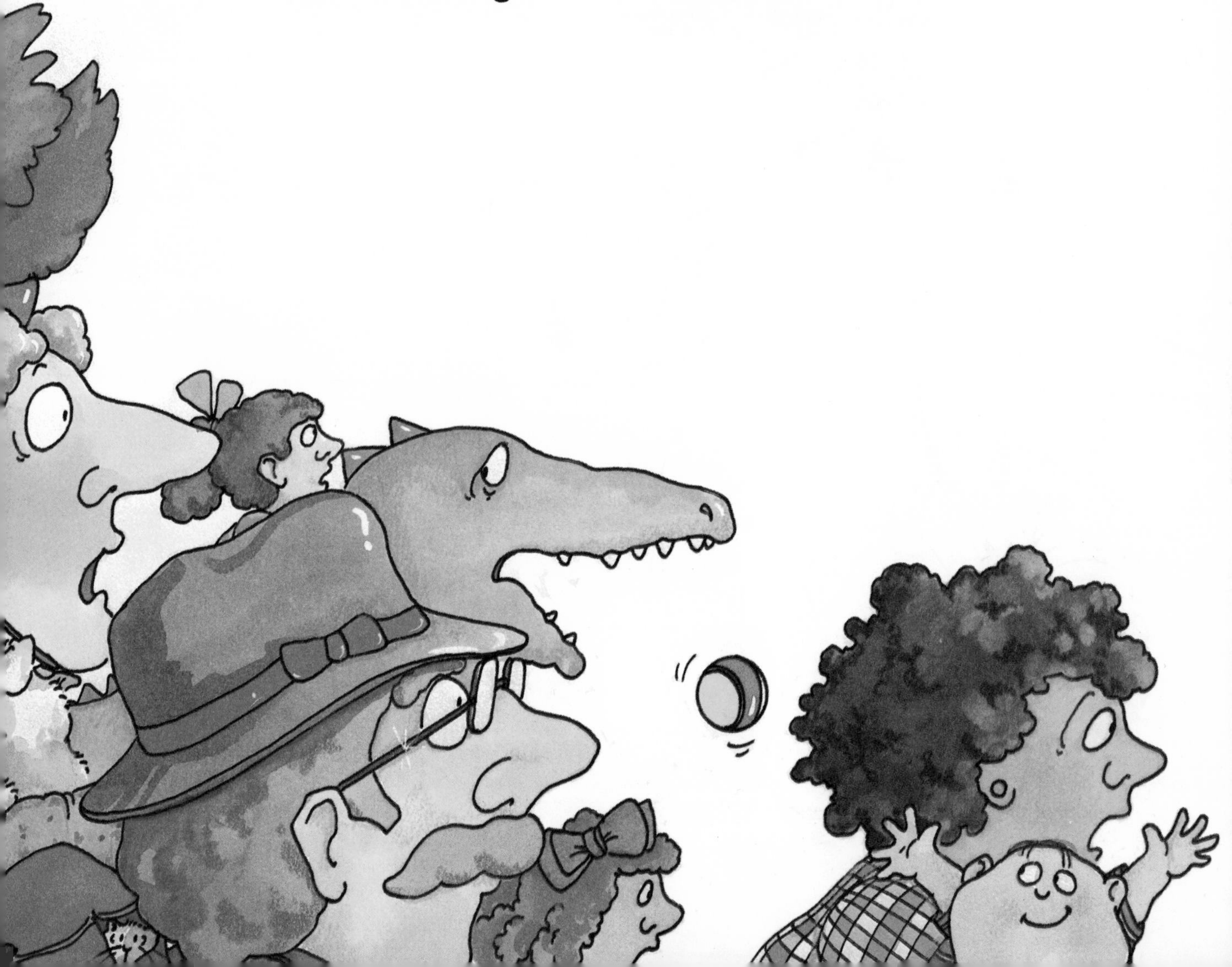

Just then, a monster in a silver suit started down the street. He had fluffy red hair and long, pointed feet.

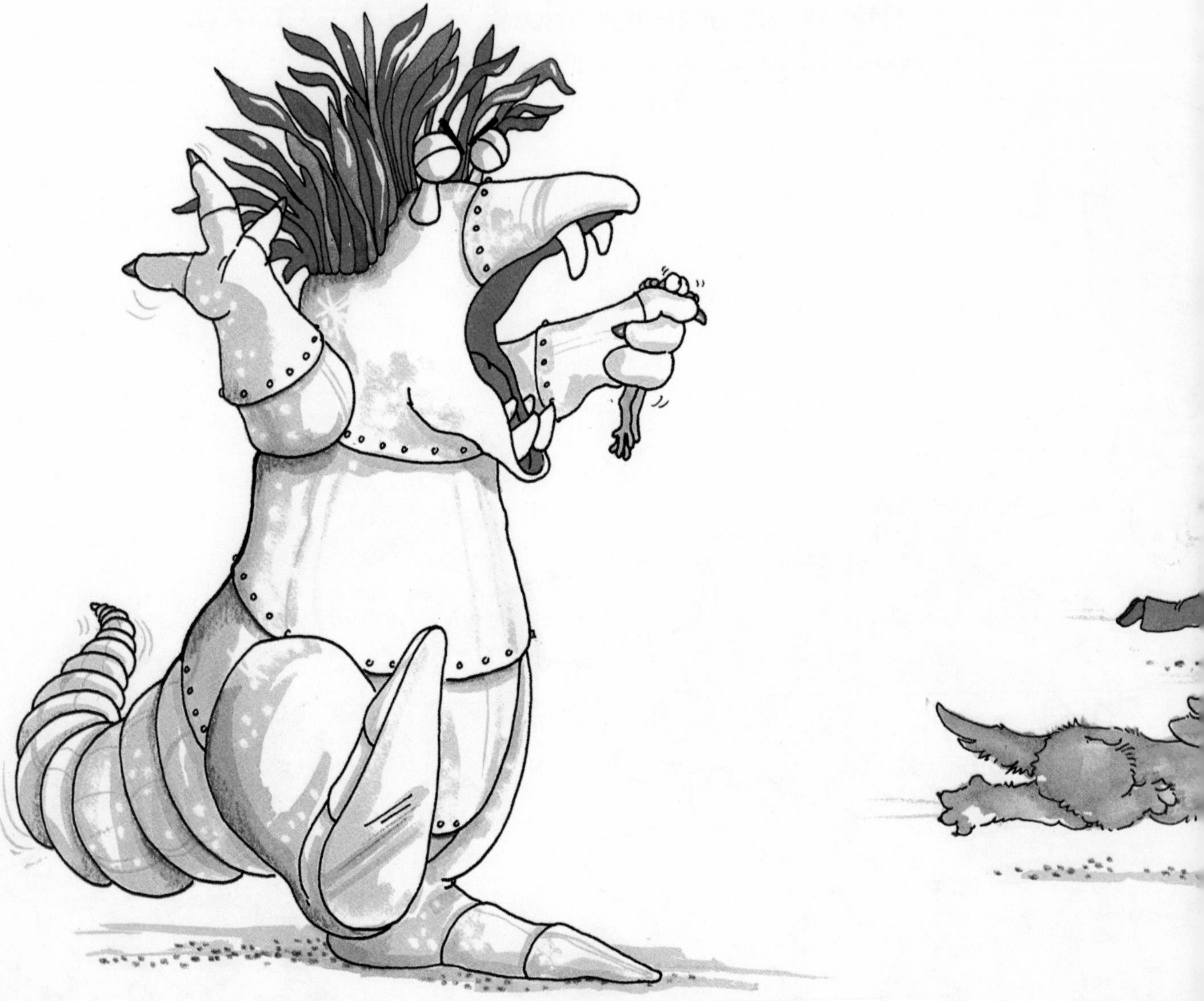

"There he is!" screamed Mr. Crown. "It's the creature from Saturn. Run before he turns us into frogs!"

Everybody ran away. Everybody but Funnyman.

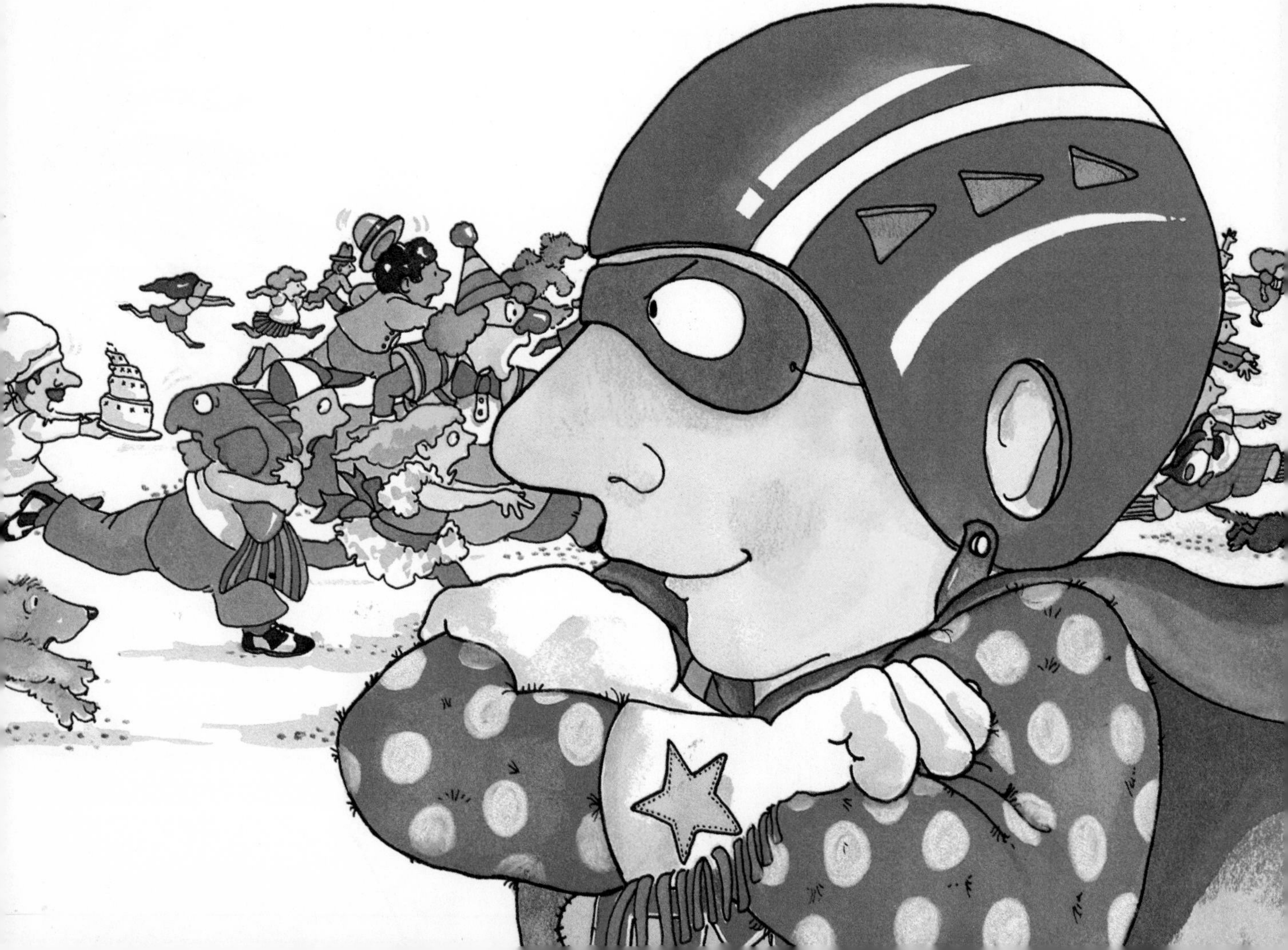

Funnyman stood in the doorway of the bank and waited for the monster. Before long, the creature came up to the door. He opened his hand and showed Funnyman a frog.

"This frog used to be the mayor," he said. "If you don't get out of my way, I'll turn you into a frog, too."

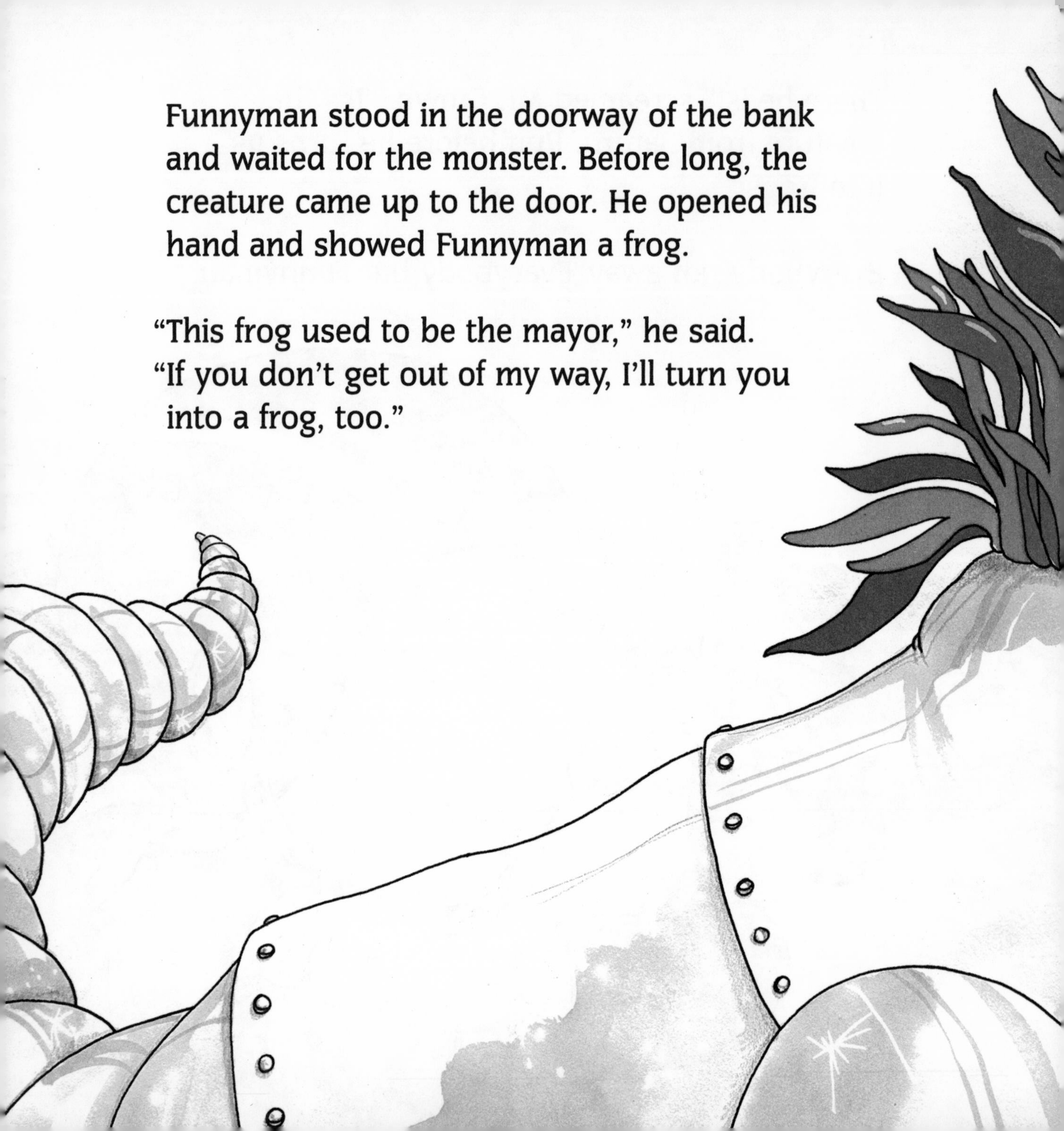

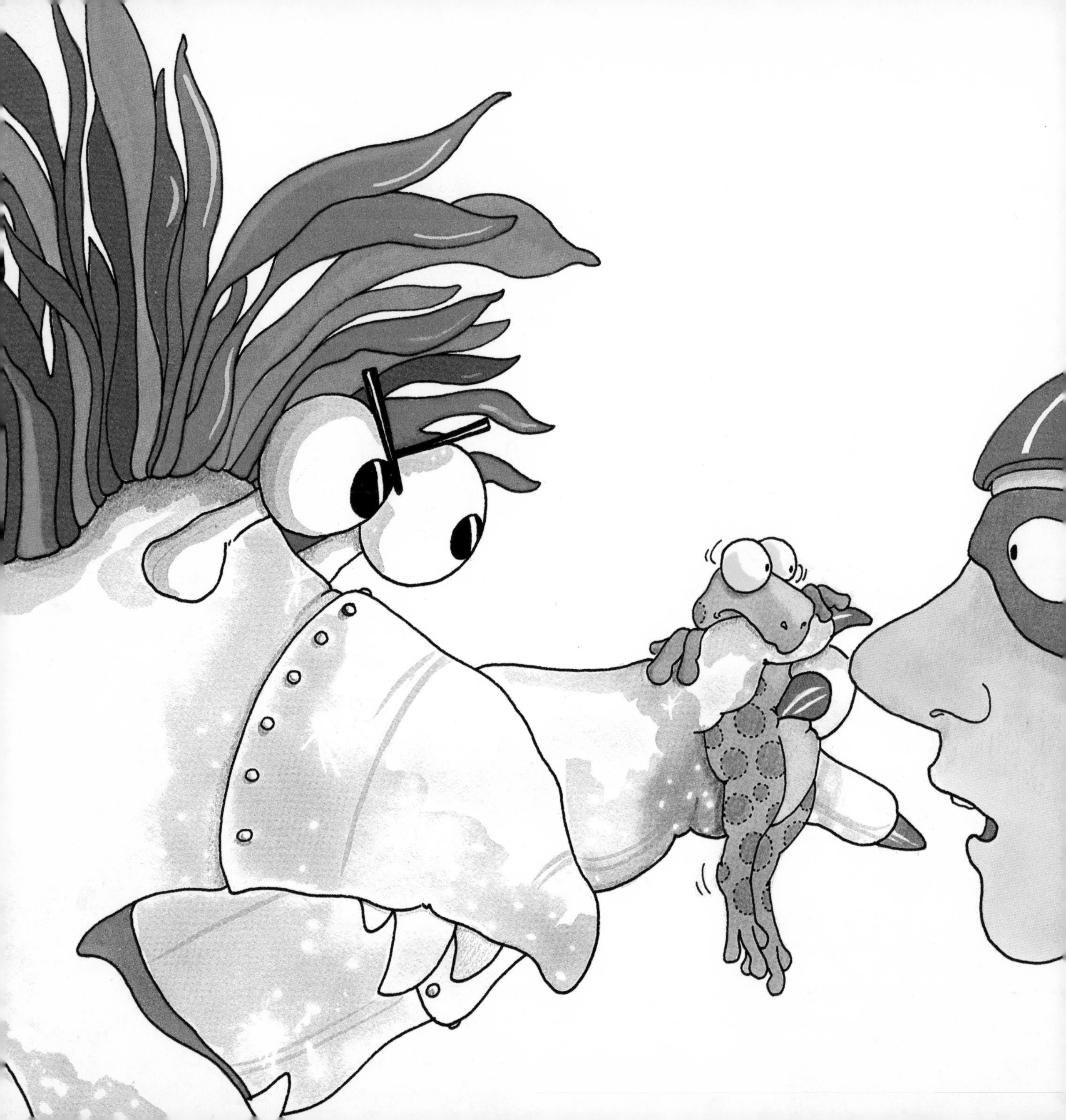

Funnyman rolled his eyes. "If you turned me into a frog, I'd croak for sure."

"Then you'd better get out of my way—and fast," said the creature.

"I'll move," said Funnyman. "But first, you must answer a riddle."

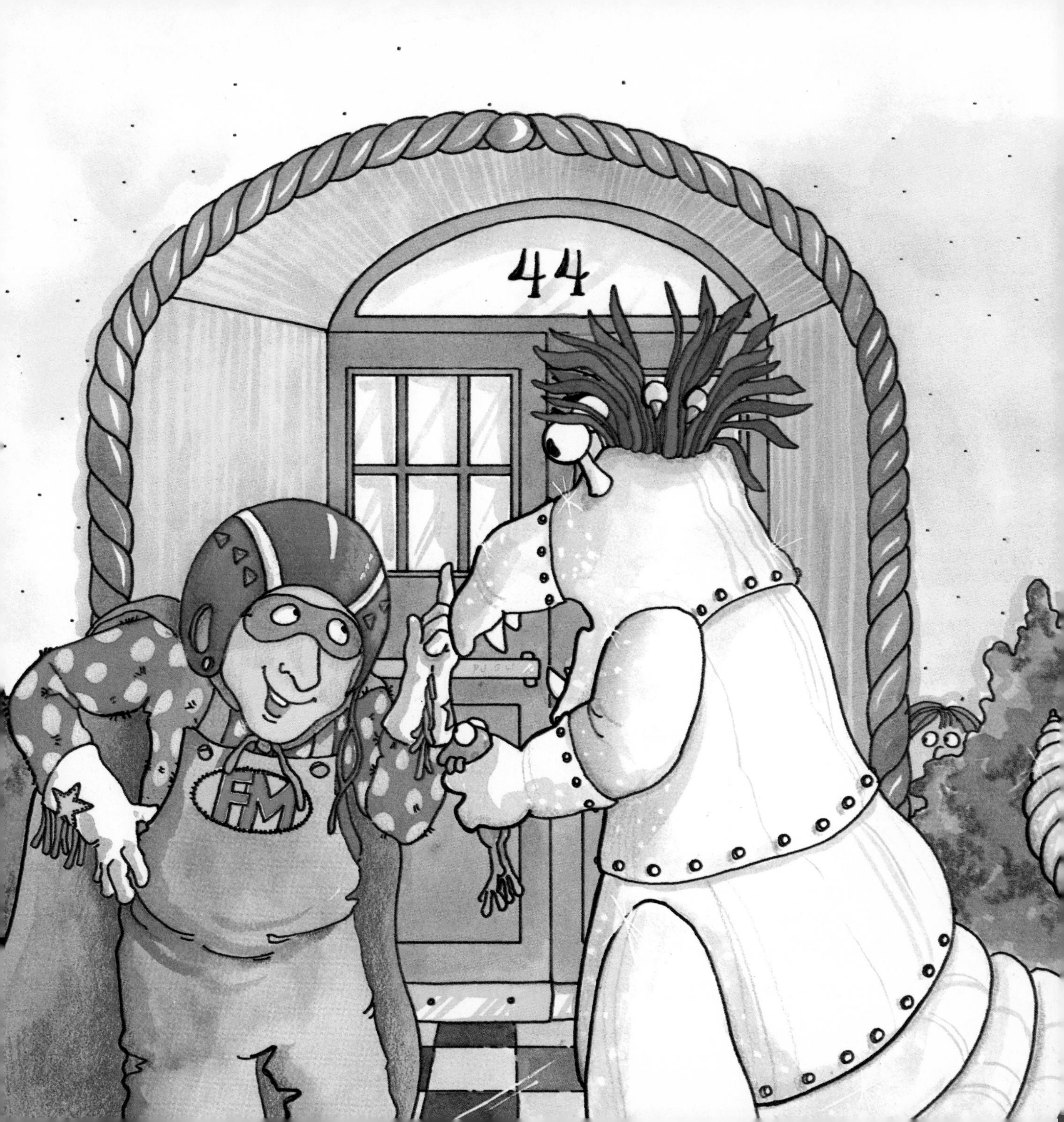
44
FM

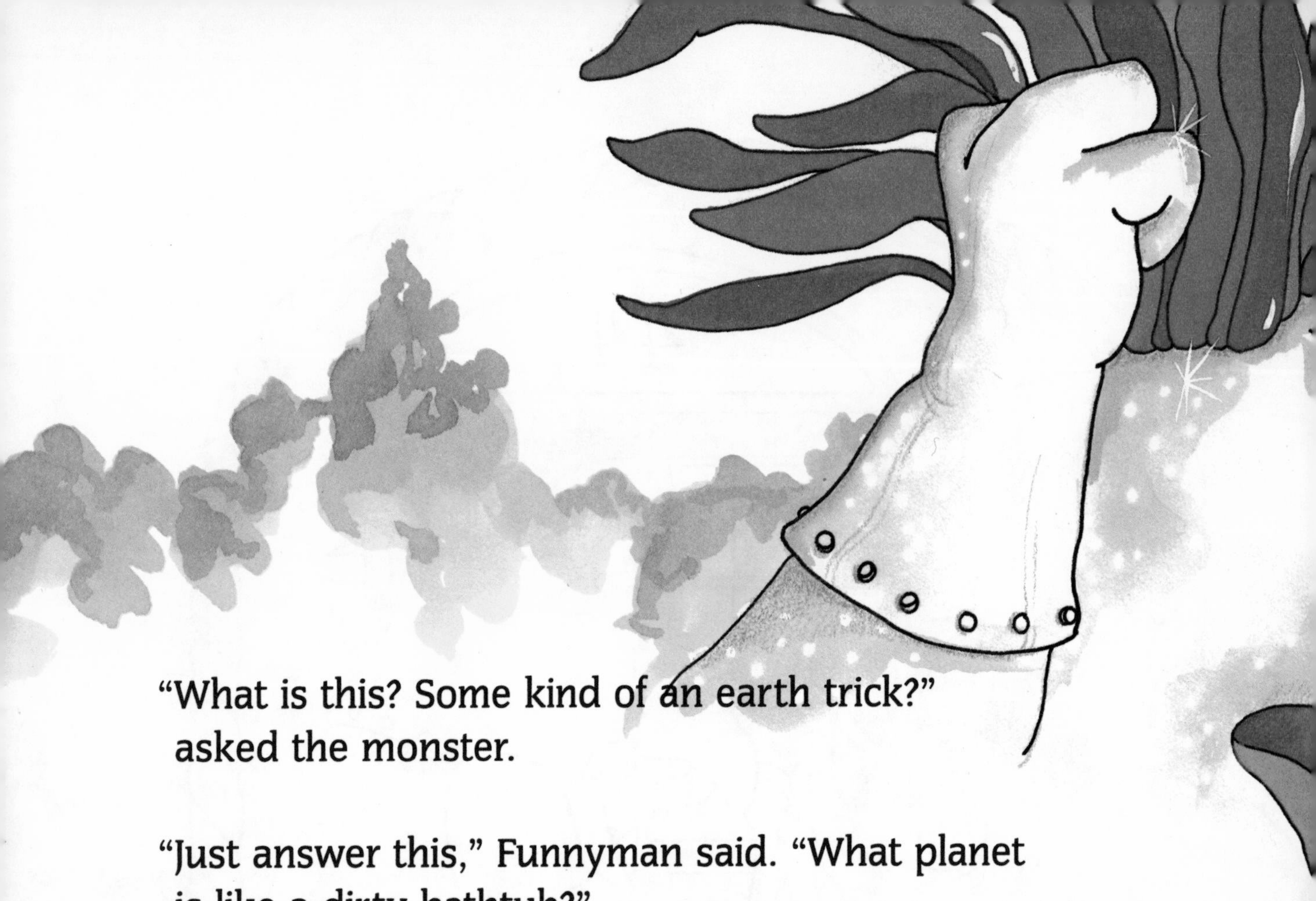

"What is this? Some kind of an earth trick?" asked the monster.

"Just answer this," Funnyman said. "What planet is like a dirty bathtub?"

The creature scratched his red hair. "What are you trying to do?" he asked. "Make a fool out of me?"

"Why should I take all the credit?" said Funnyman. "What's wrong? Don't you know the answer?"

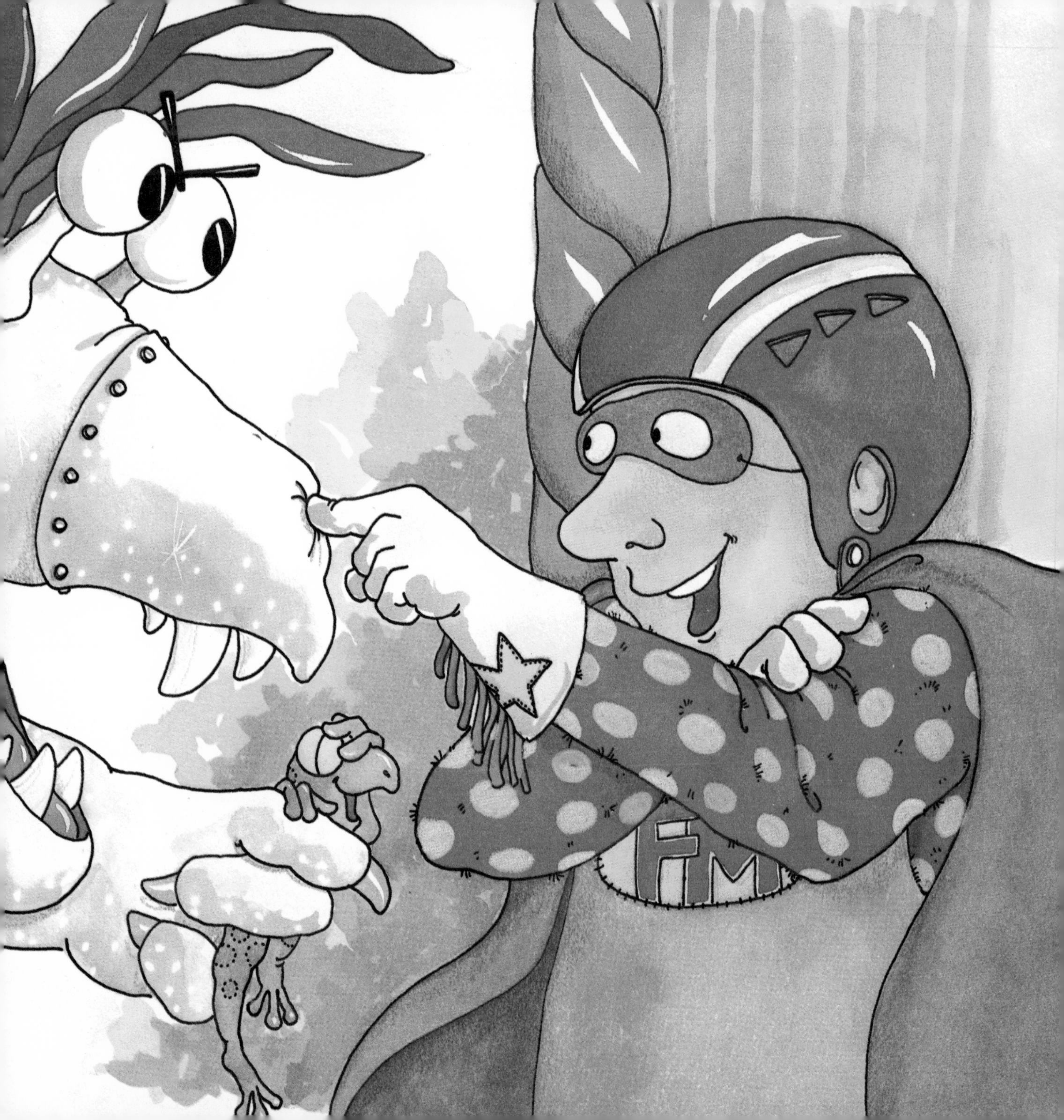
FM

"How about a clue?" asked the monster.

"Well," said Funnyman, "a dirty bathtub has a ring around it. Does that help?"

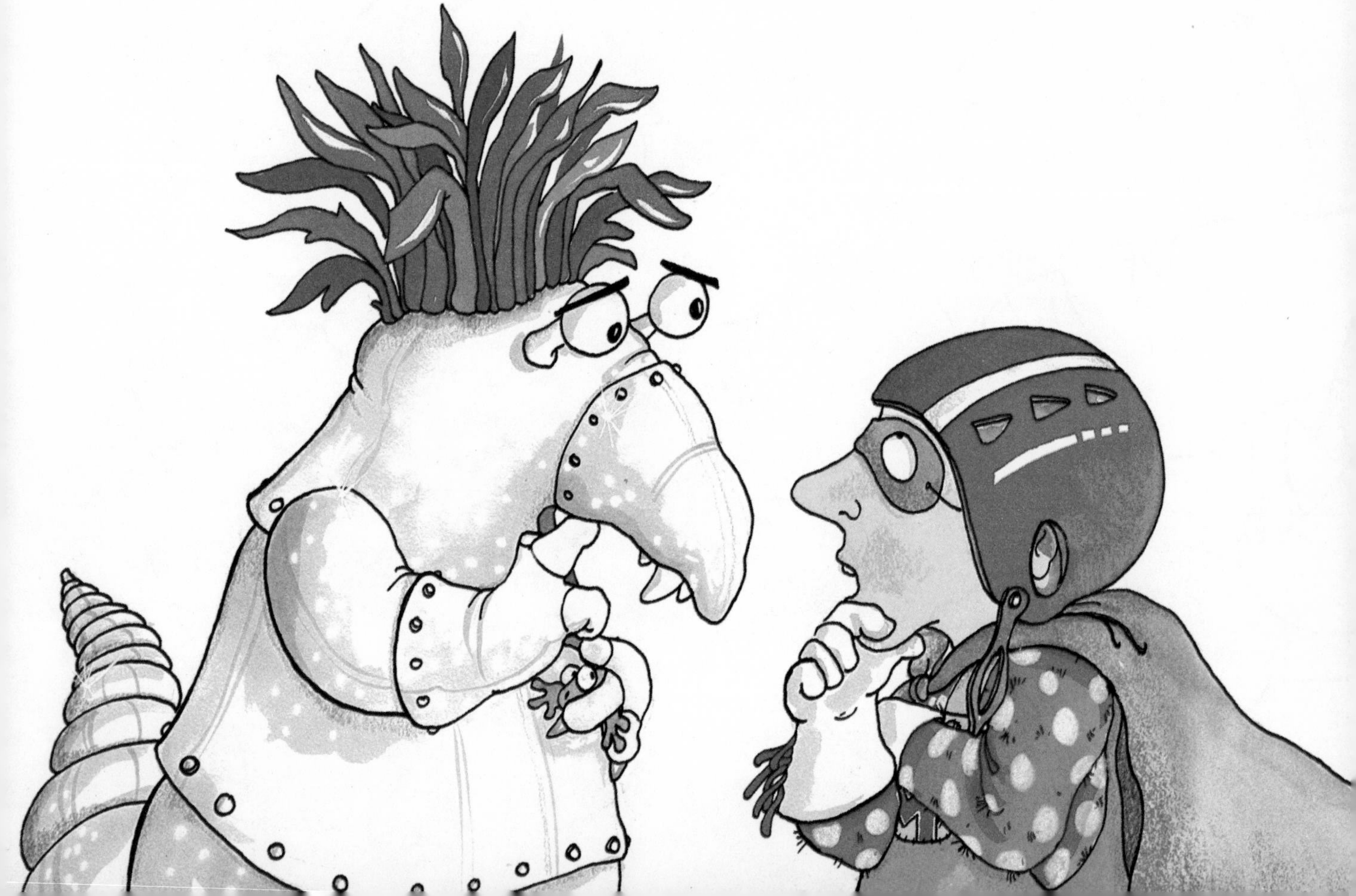

"Is the answer Mars?" asked the monster hopefully.

"Mars!" Funnyman laughed. "You are wrong! That proves you are not from Saturn."

And with that, he reached up and pulled off the mask that the creature was wearing.

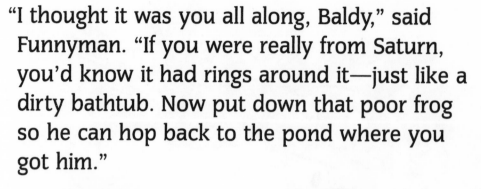

"I thought it was you all along, Baldy," said Funnyman. "If you were really from Saturn, you'd know it had rings around it—just like a dirty bathtub. Now put down that poor frog so he can hop back to the pond where you got him."

Before long, Mr. Crown came back, and so did a policewoman.

"Baldy just wanted to scare everyone away," explained Funnyman. "Then he was going to rob the bank."

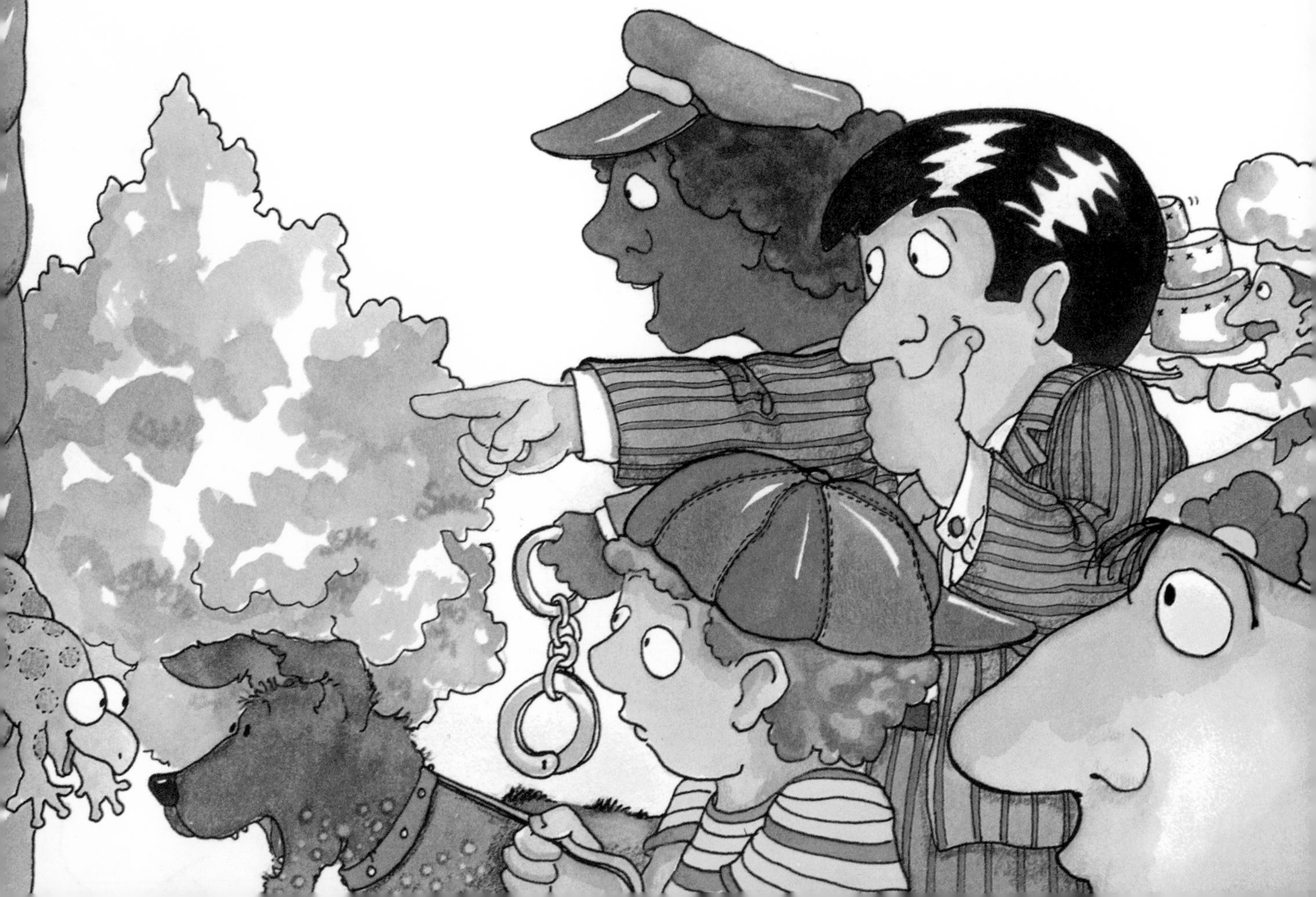

Mr. Crown shook Funnyman's hand and said, "I owe you a lot. Thanks for stopping Baldy."

"It was nothing," said Funnyman.

Then Funnyman laughed. "You could say I'm just like the hair Baldy used to have."

"What do you mean?" asked Mr. Crown.

"We both come out on top!" Funnyman said.

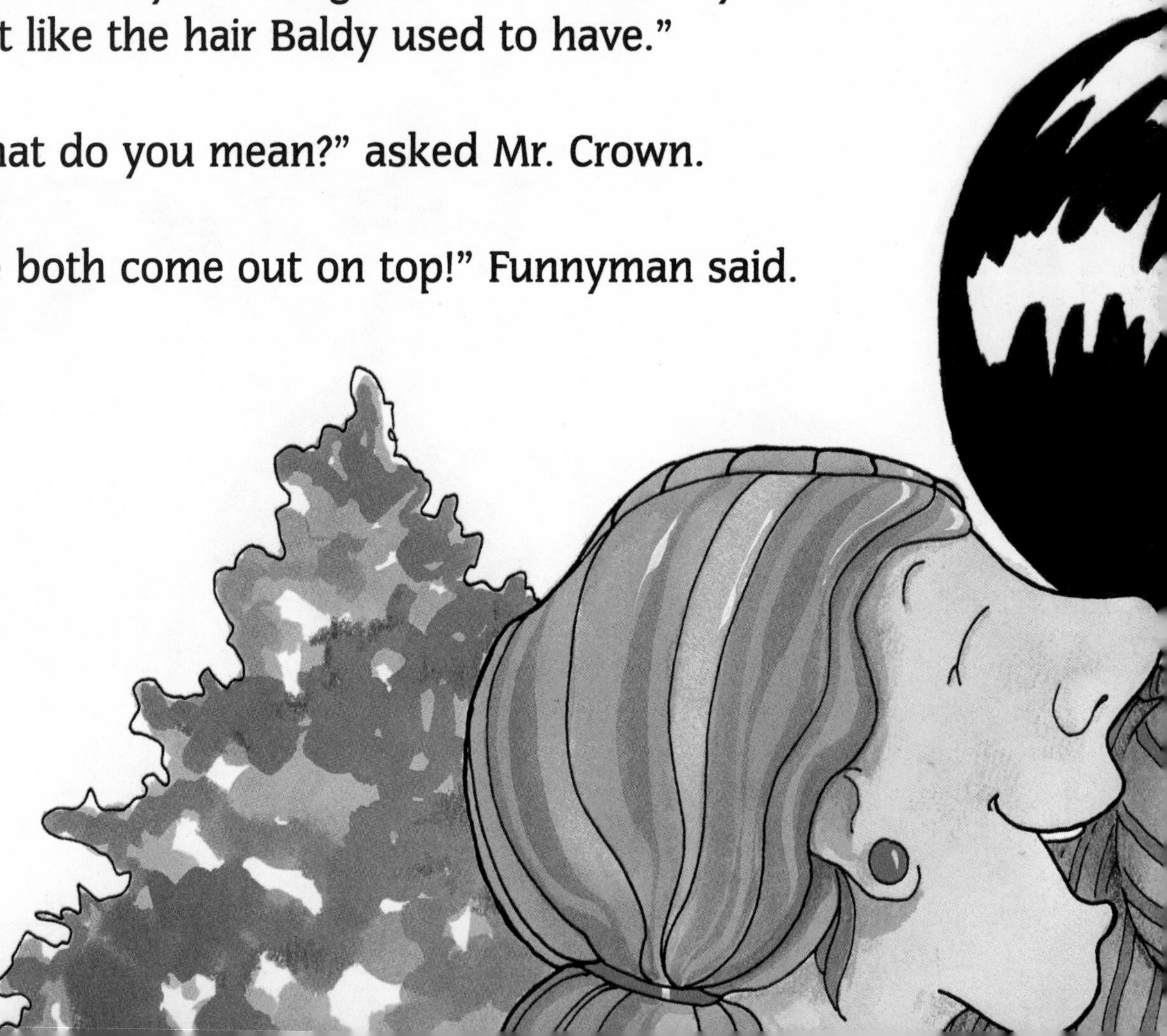

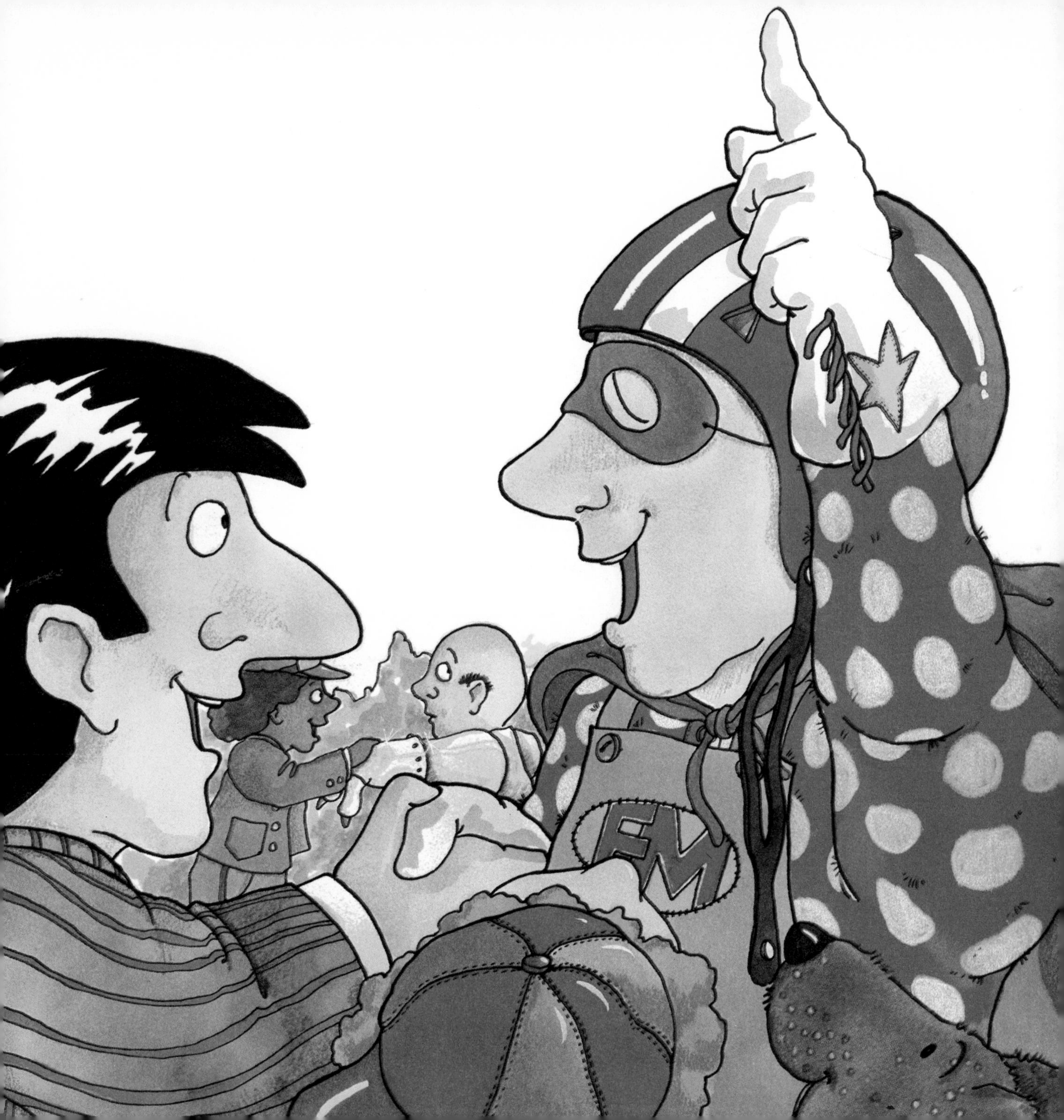
FM

Baldy rubbed his shiny head and smiled. Even he had to admit that Funnyman told great jokes.